Broken Vows

Curley A. West

&

Parson's Porch Books

www.parsonsporchbooks.com

Broken Vows

ISBN: Softcover 978-1-949888-66-9

Author Photo Credit: Amber Howze

This book is a work of fiction. All characters, incidents and dialogue are from the author's imagination or used in a fictitious manner. Any resemblance to actual persons, living or dead, or actual events is purely coincidental.

Broken Vows

Contents

Acknowledgements

First, I would like to thank God for giving me the opportunity to write this story. I would like to thank my wonderful husband DeWayne, for always being there for me. He is the love of my life and my number one fan. I am thankful for my children, mother, godmother, family and friends for all of your support and love through the years. I pray that this is the first of many books to come. Several topics are covered in this book. Many people face these circumstances. Each decision we make has a consequence. While this book is a work of fiction, I pray that it helps someone that may be going through the same things that the characters in the book experience. Lastly, I want to thank the readers. I hope you enjoy the story.

Introduction

Nothing could have prepared Shannah for what she just saw. Her husband and this woman were checking into a local hotel together. Ezekiel told me he would be working late but I guess he made a stop first. After 6 faithful years of marriage to Ezekiel, I find text messages and phone numbers to this random chick (or so I thought). I know I shouldn't have gone through his phone, but his strange behavior made me suspicious, so I began following him. I saw with my own eyes what had been distracting him. My whole life crumbled right before my eyes. What about our children? What about the vows we took? After all I have done for him, and this is how he thanks me. I was ANGRY! In the middle of my madness, Desmond sends me a message on social media. What a convenient time for my ex boyfriend to try to get in touch with me. Will Shannah forgive Ezekiel or get even?

The Beginning of Something Beautiful

My name is Shannah. I want to share with you my life story. From a child and into adulthood, I have always had trouble in my love life until I met Ezekiel. Ezekiel and I met in church. One day he walked in while the sermon was taking place. I lost focus of what the minister was saying at that point. I felt an instant attraction to this man. It was something that I had never experienced before. Once our eyes connected, it was as if we had known each other our entire lives. There is an old saying, "love at first sight". If that statement is true, then that is what happened with us. I know we should have had our mind on God while we were in church, but we did not. As soon as service was over, he walked over to the end of the pew where I was standing. Ezekiel had gray eyes that pierced at your heart when you looked at him. He had thick black eyelashes that were perfect. It was as if he was staring into my soul. It sent shock waves throughout me. My heart was pounding, and my palms were sweaty. I had so many emotions flowing through me. It is hard to explain. It did not hurt that he was 6 foot 5 inches tall and bulging biceps everywhere. He was very easy on the eye. He had thick, sandy brown wavy hair. His skin was the color of bronze. He looked like a model or someone very important. He didn't have a blemish anywhere and his skin was flawless. He appeared to be athletic or he worked out on a regular basis. You wouldn't think he would want to talk with someone like me because I wasn't the prettiest girl. I was bullied my whole life about my looks. Because of this, I was self conscious about my looks and appearance. People called me ugly and children teased me constantly. To be honest with you, I felt ugly. As an adult, people continue to talk down to me. I try to be a peaceful person, so I just do not say anything or walk away. I have severe eczema and acne. I had a honey colored complexion, 5 foot 11 inches tall, with long hair that reached to my waistline. I was proud of my hair. It was thick and wavy. I didn't know how to style my hair, so I basically wore it in a pony tail and wore clothing that wasn't age appropriate. The only thing I had going for myself were my big flawless legs. That was the only thing I ever received compliments on besides my wonderful personality and big heart. I also dressed more like an older adult. I didn't have a figure. My best friend Miranda fought many fights defending me. Miranda often reminded me that my wardrobe was outdated. I didn't listen to Miranda because I didn't feel like she would understand. Miranda was dark skinned, 40-24-40 were her measurements. She had what the people called a Coca-Cola bottle figure. Her skin was flawless, and she always had some guy chasing behind her. We were so opposite it would be hard to believe we were friends. She was more like a sister than a friend. When Ezekiel started to talk to me, I was taken back at first. Miranda was usually the one the guys liked. I really did not know what to think. I had stopped drooling over him long enough to hold a conversation. When we talked, it was if no one else existed. We were in our own little world. We exchanged numbers and not long after, Ezekiel joined my church. It was kind of scary that we had so much in common. He and I loved to read. I could get lost in a story. If a story was really good, I could finish a book in a day. Reading was always relaxing for me and it made me forget about problems or things that I may have been experiencing at the moment. We both loved history and had a passion for cooking. Ezekiel was surprised that I loved to hunt and fish. He said he never took me for that type. I told him he could thank my dad for that. My dad even made sure I learned to change a tire because he did not want me off somewhere stranded. Ezekiel and I loved people. We would go out of our way to help anyone. Ezekiel shared with me that he loved the fact that I wasn't like typical females my age. I wasn't focused 100% on my outward appearance. He said I had a sparkle in my eyes, and I stood out in a crowd because I had an inner glow and compassion. Ezekiel said he saw love when he looked at me and I never met a stranger. He said he knew I was self-conscious about my appearance, but I shouldn't be. He said he loved everything about me, and I had a beautiful heart and mind. Those things were priceless. Ezekiel always flattered me with his words. He had a way of talking that could put at ease. My mind went back to my childhood. I was always told as a child and even into adulthood that I had a special spirit and God didn't bless everyone with the gift that he had blessed me with. My main problem was that I was gullible. I knew that this was my weakness. I think this was why I never had relationships that would work out. My cousin always told me I would buy ice in Alaska. I tried to see good in everyone. When I was with Ezekiel, he made me feel good about myself. I felt confident. He was always encouraging me to be a better person. It wasn't long before I was falling for Ezekiel. I didn't want to be away from him any longer than I had to be. After the all-night phone conversations and spending all of our free time together, we both were head over hills in love.

We never wanted to hang up the phone. We would go back and forth for hours debating over who would hang up the phone first. Sometimes we would fall asleep on the phone. We were both only 24, but after a series of failed relationships for both of us, there looked like there may be some hope for real love after all.

The Proposal

After only six months of dating, Ezekiel proposed to me. I know a lot of people think that some people move to fast when it comes to marriage. My parents would always tell me, "it is better to marry than burn, the bible tells us that". And I know we have all heard the expression, "why buy the cow when you can get the milk for free".

My parents were encouraging me to wait to have sex when I am married. I had other people to tell me, "You should test drive a car before you buy it". That was why they had sex outside of marriage and they would know whether they wanted to get married. I was old fashioned though. I was going to wait for Mr. Right and he would be my one and only. Mr. Right would never cheat on me and would always put my needs ahead of his own. I would shower him with all the love I could possibly give, and we would live happily ever after. At least that was what I thought true love was.

Ezekiel was my Mr. Right and I would be is Mrs. Right. The day he proposed to me is a day I will never forget. It wasn't your typical proposal. He didn't put a ring in my glass at a restaurant or put it on a billboard. He did something out of the ordinary. During the announcements at church, he raised his hand and said he had to make an announcement. I was wondering what he needed to say. We had a clerk that handled the announcements at church. So it was strange that Ezekiel stood up to make an announcement. He looked over to where I was sitting and began to smile. I smiled back at him.

Ezekiel had that effect on me. When he smiled, I forgot about anything that may have been troubling me. His piercing eyes are one thing I loved about him. I felt love every time I looked at him. Ezekiel begins to tell the audience that he was inviting them to his wedding. This got my attention because the congregation knew he and I were dating. My mind suddenly drifted back to Devon. Devon and I dated for about a year.

During that year, he joined the military and was gone the majority of our relationship. He was older than I was, but he was in the church as well. Devon told me that he would save his money and marry me after he had served time in the military. He asked me to wait on him. I agreed to wait while he went away to make a better future for us. He wrote me letters and sent me pictures. I wrote him back and mailed pictures too. He called me as much as he could.

After basic training, he came home, and we spent time together until he had to go away again. I was young and foolish enough to believe what he said. His aunt approached me after a function one night to let me know he had gotten married. My heart instantly broke.

I kept my composure until I got in the car and told my mom and dad what had happened. I cried all the way home that night. I did not sleep that night. The next day, Devon called, and I asked him was it true. He told me no and assured me that he loved only me. But I never heard from him anymore after that. To this day,

I never understood why Devon had me believing a lie that he told. I have never had any luck in the love department. Just before I could get too deep in thoughts from my past, Ezekiel brought me out of my daydreaming. He was walking toward where I was sitting. My heart begins to race, I was perspiring like crazy. I was wondering what he was doing. He then said to the congregation, you would have to ask Shannah about the date and time of their wedding.

I was confused at this point, but Ezekiel pulled out a silver ring with several diamonds embedded around the entire band. It had one large ruby in the center. He got down on one knee and asked me to marry him. He said the reason it was one ruby in the ring was because it was unique and beautiful just as I was. He fell in love with me not because I was like everyone else but because I was special and different. He promised me he would never hurt me and wanted to spend the rest of his life proving that to me. Tears of joy filled my eyes. No person had ever told me those things. I happily accepted his proposal.

I thought it was so romantic for him to propose to me in church because that is where we met. There was not a dry eye in the church. Everyone came up and congratulated us after service. This was one of the best days of my life. I finally had my Mr. Right.

Ezekiel and I choose to remain celibate until we became married. It was not hard for me to do because I was still a virgin. Ezekiel was not a virgin but vowed to wait until marriage before he had sex again. He said he wanted our first time together to be special and I would be the only woman for him for the rest of our lives.

The Vows

My best friend, Miranda and I began planning the wedding. Miranda had been my best friend since Kindergarten. She knew me better than I knew myself. Miranda was the opposite of everything I was. She was beautiful, a body to kill for and confident. I wish I had the strength she possessed.

No one ever took advantage of her. She said exactly what was on her mind and never sugar coated the truth. Her favorite quote to me was, "just because you are saved, you don't have to let people run over you". She was going to be my maid of honor. Since she was better at planning events than I was, she took control of the wedding and reception planning.

I was more than happy to give her that task. I knew nothing about how to put together invitations, programs or decorations. Miranda was always looking out for me and I loved her for that. She was my sister from another mother. She loved the fact that Ezekiel seemed to genuinely love me. I had bad luck when it came to dating.

It seemed like I always picked the wrong guy. When men found out that I was not going to sleep with them, they broke up with me. Sam comes to mind. He was a young man that I loved once. He always hung around and talked to me on a daily basis. He let me in on the games that boys play, and he was easy to talk too. We were friends for about two years before we dated briefly.

His female friend Imani hung around him too much for my liking. I always asked him about her, but he denied anything other than friendship. Imani had a cute face and yes of course, she had a big bootie too. I took Sam for his word when he said she was only a friend and he only had eyes for me. Imani and her friend, Khadejah always made fun of me when they thought I was not looking or listening. I thought Imani liked Sam and she had Khadejah to pick at me because of it. I remember when he asked me to go to the prom with him. I was so excited. The theme was always and forever.

I remembered dancing to this song on the dance floor and thought that we would be together forever. Sam suggested we walk outside to get away from some of the noise of the prom and I agreed. He asked me to sit in the car with him to talk. I was so trustworthy of him because I knew Sam was a good person and would never do anything to hurt me. What harm could come from talking. When we got to the car, he suggested we sit in the back seat to have more room. After getting in the back seat with Sam, he jumped on top of me. I begin to scream and yelled to him that we weren't talking, and I didn't want to do anything else, but he ignored me. I was scared and then I hear pounding on the window. It was Miranda. He got off me and let me out of the car. Miranda slapped Sam across his face for trying to take advantage of me, and she scolded me for going off with him. She then took my hand and dragged me back into the prom.

She acted more like my mother that night. Now that I think about it, that wasn't a very good idea, but I can laugh at it now. I always tried to see the good in everyone. That was one reason I fell in love with Ezekiel because he never tried to take advantage of my kindness. Miranda and he got along great. Ezekiel and I got along with each other's family too. That made our relationship even better. We choose the day of love to get married.

Our Valentine's Day wedding ceremony was beautiful. The colors were red and white. I chose a sleeveless, simple, white floor length gown. The edges of my neckline and bottom of the dress were diamonds. I wore a diamond tiara with one ruby in the center that had a veil attached to it that covered my face. My hair was pulled up on top of my head in curls. I wore my great grandmother's diamond solitaire earrings. Miranda and I had a spa day before the wedding and my skin was flawless. She hired a professional make-up artist. I wanted to look perfect for Ezekiel and I did. He wore a black and white tuxedo and white accessories.

He looked like an angel standing in the front of the church. When I walked down the aisle, all I could see was Ezekiel. He had my undivided attention and I had his. We wrote our own vows to each other. We took vows to love, honor and cherish through sickness, and in health, till death do us part. I couldn't wait to start my new life with Ezekiel and live happily ever after.

Life after marriage

In the beginning of our marriage, everything was perfect. I catered to Ezekiel and he catered to me. Anyone around us could feel the love we shared for one another. I always made sure everything at home was perfect. I kept the house spotless and I cooked. It was not microwave food, but it was home cooked, five course meals. I served Ezekiel because he was my king. He never had a worry because I made sure he did not. I even laid his clothing out for him for the day. I did these things because I loved him, and he made me feel loved in return.

Ezekiel would always shower me with gifts and affection. It did not have to be a special occasion and that is what I loved about his gestures. He left love notes on the refrigerator, in the bathroom and sometimes he left them in my car. I would always find one at the perfect moment. They made me smile. It came in handy especially if I was having a rough day. He always made sure I had money in my accounts. He kept the yards maintained at home. Ezekiel made sure my car was serviced and detailed.

If he made it home before I did, he would cook and serve me. I would go out to the car in the morning to head to work and it was a note on my seat that he had left. He not only told me he loved me, he would show it in so many ways. I could not have asked for a better man. I remember when I found out I was pregnant. Miranda was picking at me about my hips starting to spread. She joked that if I did not watch it, I would soon be as voluptuous as she was. I just laughed.

Miranda knew she had it going on and maybe one day I would have the same confidence as she had. I had missed my period and decided to take a pregnancy test. It came back positive. I was so happy. Ezekiel and Miranda were overjoyed as well. The way the both of them catered to me, you would have thought I was fragile. My parents and in-laws did not have to worry about me because they made sure all was well. Ezekiel would rub my feet and my back and give me massages that would make me forget what pain was. He would sing to the babies and they would kick as if they were responding back to him. I was having twins. Ezekiel wanted boys but I just wanted healthy babies. He had even picked out their names, Ezekiel and Daniel. It did not matter to me if the twins were boys or girls, or even one of each. My marriage and life was as close to perfect as you could get. I was so happy and could not wait for the twins to make their entrance into the world and join our happy home. It would not take long for my dream to become a reality. On New Year's Day, we welcomed two beautiful daughters, Anna and Janna. This was a wonderful way to start a new year. Anna had green eyes and Janna had gray eyes. They were two of the most precious babies you would ever want to see.

Anna had a head full of straight hair and Janna did not have any hair at all. Ezekiel's dream of having a son did not come true, but it did not matter because he was happy. I remember him saying they had his heart already and whatever they wanted, they would get. I know Ezekiel would make sure of that. He was such a good provider and my happily ever after just got better.

A Woman's Intuition

Ezekiel and I had been married for 6 years now, but after the birth of our children, we became distant from one another. The love notes stopped. I stopped catering to him and he stopped catering to me. I did not have any energy because he did not help with the kids, as he should have. I worked a full-time job, cooked, cleaned and raised our daughters basically alone. It did not help matters that I recently suffered a miscarriage.

I was alone at the doctor's office when I found out. I had missed my cycle and went to the doctor for a checkup. When they told me the news, I was so excited. I thought that the baby would bring us closer together and Ezekiel would get the son he has always wanted. I remember looking at the baby on the ultrasound machine. I was around 8 weeks pregnant. I could not wait to get home to tell my husband the good news but that never happened. Before I could leave the doctor's office, I passed out and when I awoke, I was in the hospital with Miranda standing by my side.

When she told me, I had lost the baby, it was as if life literally rushed out of me. I began to cry. It seems like here lately; all life serves me is pain. In the midst of my tears, I looked around and noticed that my husband was not there. I asked Miranda where was Ezekiel? She said she could not reach him. That should not have surprised me. It was hard to reach him by text message or phone lately.

The miscarriage started a downward spiral of our marriage. It did not help that Ezekiel had begun coming home late from work. He drove trucks for a living but had a local route where he could come home daily. At first, I didn't think anything about it because we needed the extra income. Two children were hard to support with our incomes. I didn't make very much money working in retail.

Day care for the children took up the majority of my check and Ezekiel paid the other bills.

He begins to work overtime every day of the week. He was unable to attend church anymore. Sex did not exist anymore (if he is not getting it from me, he must be getting it somewhere). When Ezekiel did come home, he was constantly on his cell phone. I asked him who was he was texting and talking to, and that is when the arguments begin. He accused me of not trusting him.

He often reminded me that if we didn't have trust, we didn't have a marriage. He would also tell me that if I always thought he was cheating than I must be cheating. My mind drifted back to Michael. Michael was someone I dated in school briefly. He broke my heart with one of our classmates named Paris. Everyone in the school knew about the incident before I did. I asked Michael about it and he said he did have sex with Paris, but it was only a one-night stand. I can say that at least he was honest and told me. There I go letting my mind drift back to the past again. It seems as though every person that has entered my life has broken my heart. I just hope Ezekiel has not repeated the cycle. I let it go because I did not like arguing in front of our kids. I was beginning to get worried. We were not attending church as we needed and now, we are having trouble in our marriage.

I think we are heading for trouble when we leave God out of the equation. I know I had not prayed, and I do not believe Ezekiel had either. I was looking at the distractions around us. One day when Ezekiel was in the bathroom, I picked up his phone to see if I saw any suspicious activity. I needed his password to unlock it. We normally did not lock our phones. I questioned him about it, and he asked me why I was worried about his phone. I asked him was he cheating on me. He asked was I cheating on him (I hated reverse psychology). I let it go again. However, I decided to do a little investigative work. I begin snooping through his things. I didn't find anything at first. I asked myself if I was cheating, where I would hide things. The answer is in plain sight. It came to me to look in his man cave.

In the corner to the back of the room was a toolbox. I opened it and there were his check stubs (he told me he was registered online at his job and did not get paper stubs anymore), along with another cell phone I knew nothing about). There was no over time on any of his checks. The cell phones were full of texts, pictures and phone calls from a female. She looked so familiar but right now I was so angry. I couldn't think straight. I knew I would have to catch Ezekiel in the act because there was no way he was confessing to anything. My mother always told me if you go looking for something you will find it. I was about to start looking.

The Broken Vows

Today would be my first attempt to see if Ezekiel is cheating on me. I had mixed feelings. It's so hard to believe that I'm even in this position. I still remember our wedding day. What happened to Ezekiel and me? After the birth of our twins, we did not spend any quality time together. I put all of my energy into the kids and so did he. I wish now we could have made more time for one another. I realize now the impact it had on our marriage.

I hope Ezekiel is not doing wrong but I am going to find out. I took a day off from my job. I put on a wig, some shades, and some old clothes and jumped in my rental car. I went to Ezekiel's job and waited across the street in the parking lot. He came out to his car on his lunch break, but he wasn't alone (I thought this was strange because I packed him a lunch every night). He was with a beautiful woman. I didn't think anything about it at first, until they got in his truck and drove out of the parking lot. The woman looked so familiar (it was the same woman that he had pictures of).

I begin to shake. I was angry. I still gave him the benefit of doubt. Maybe she needed a ride somewhere. Maybe this was a relative. I was already making assumptions and did not have all the facts yet. I put my emotions to the side and decided to follow them. Several things came to my mind while I was driving. I was lost for words at this point. I started with happily ever after. I am now following my husband to see if he is having an affair. I followed them for about ten minutes, and they came to a stop. My heart rate went up at this point. They pulled up in front of a hotel. Why were they were here? Why were they together?

Ezekiel walked over and opened her car door. She stepped out of the vehicle and grabbed his hand. They walked hand in hand to the front door of the lobby. When they walked past my car, that's when the tears begin to flow. It was big booty Keisha. Keisha and I had been friends from elementary through high school.

She was always the popular girl in school. Her nickname was big booty Keisha. She was light-skinned and had honey brown eyes, and a short blond hairstyle. She was wearing 5-inch stilettos with a daisy dukes and a off the shoulder cropped blouse. She looked absolutely stunning.

We lost touch after graduation, but she knew Ezekiel was my husband, because we had contact with each other over the years. Keisha was also married to Ted. I wonder what Ted would think if he saw what I was seeing now. Ezekiel and Keisha walked back by my car, they embraced and went into the room. I cried and cried and cried. I didn't know what else to do. I thought about the wedding vows we took, our kids. Before I knew it, I had sat there for an hour. I thought about killing them both. I had a loaded gun sitting on the seat next to me. I could put a bullet in them both but that would only land me in jail.

As I was thinking, my phone buzzed letting me know I had a social media notification. I looked and it was a message from my ex boyfriend, Desmond. What a convenient time for him to message me. I opened the message up and it was innocent, he only asked how I was doing. I couldn't decide whether to respond or not because of the crisis that just erupted in my marriage, so I decided not to say anything to Desmond.

I decided to walk up to the hotel room door. On my way to the door, I took out my pocket knife and slashed holes in Ezekiel's tires. I stood outside of the door and listened as Kiesha and Ezekiel made love. Tears began to flow again. But this time they were tears of rage. I began to bang on the door until Ezekiel opened it. I ran in and begin throwing punches at Kiesha. I have never been a fighter, but I threw one punch after another. I took out all of the rage that had built up on the inside of me out on Kiesha. She didn't have a chance to defend herself. Ezekiel tried to pull me off of her, but he couldn't. I then begin to throw punches at Ezekiel. I felt like he was defending Kiesha. He was begging me to calm down.

Security came to the room and finally restrained me. They offered to call the police. Keisha immediately said she didn't want the police involved, and she wouldn't press any charges because she didn't want her husband to find out (I was speechless at this point). She took off running out of the room.

I turned my back to Ezekiel (he was apologizing and crying) and left the hotel and went to the turn in my rental car. I didn't expect to find anything on Ezekiel so quickly. I guess my mother was right and I found what I was looking for. Things would never be the same from this day forward.

Shannah's Aftermath

I went to school, picked up the girls, and headed to a hotel. Anna and Janna wondered where their daddy was. It is sad when parents go through hard times and there are kids involved. They never understand what is going on.

I can relate because I went through so many things in my childhood. The girls had grown up so fast. Anna had a head full of short tight curly locks and had a light complexion. She was a bundle of energy. Anna was very outspoken and would stare at you as if she could see your soul. Janna was brown skinned with freckles. She was very shy and kept mostly to herself. She had straight brown hair. Even though they were sisters and twins, they were opposite like day and night. Anna was a lot like her dad and Janna was a lot like me. Anna would debate everything I told her, and Janna would accept everything I said.

They both did whatever Ezekiel asked without debate. I loved them both so much. I tried to protect them from any and everything. I did not want to bad mouth their father to them so I told them we were having a mommy and daughter's night out and they would see him on tomorrow. The girls did not pry and ask any more questions. I keep an extra bag of clothes in my car (for me and the girls because they were always messing up their clothing and mine too) so I didn't have to go home. Ezekiel must have called me a hundred times. I ignored all of his calls. I needed some time to think and process what had happened today and what I would do. Lucky for me, the girls had a long day and went to sleep quickly. I powered my phone off and went to sleep. Beating up Keisha and Ezekiel had worn me out.

The next day I dropped the girls off to school. I called my job and took the remainder of the week off. I never missed work, so I had maxed out on vacation time and I had a good boss, so no questions were asked. My boss was always telling me to take some time off, so what better time to take him up on his offer. I went to the salon and got a complete makeover. I cut off all 32 inches of my hair. I got a short-layered style.

I went to the mall and asked for help from the associate. I told her I wanted a new wardrobe. She looked at me and said she was happy to help. I got a new wardrobe, jewelry, and shoes to match. Thank God I had Ezekiel's credit card to fund my shopping trip and makeover. I usually kept it for emergencies, and this was an emergency. I went and got a manicure, pedicure and a facial. Today would be all about me. I had even more insecurities now that Ezekiel had cheated on me. I felt like I wasn't good enough. I even went and purchased a fake butt (don't laugh).

I never had a butt and maybe if my butt were bigger, Ezekiel would not have chased after Kiesha. At least that's what I thought at the moment. Maybe I should have taken better care of my appearance. I really did not put a lot of effort into fixing myself up. When I think back, I could have kept my hair and nails done.

I also could have tried to mix and match some of my clothing to look more my age. I just put so much time into taking care of the kids and keeping the house in order until I let myself go. Miranda was always fussing about me not putting any effort into keeping my appearance intact. She often fussed and reminded me to put some gloss on those crusty lips of yours. Maybe I should have listened. Was it my fault Ezekiel felt the need to go outside of our marriage to have his needs fulfilled? So many things were running through my mind. I mostly blamed myself.

I picked the girls up from school and decided to head home to face the drama. I turned my phone back on and yes, Ezekiel had called so many times that my voicemail was full. I decided to call Miranda to fill her in on what had happened. She had sent several text messages since I wasn't answering my phone.

Ezekiel went to her home looking for me and the girls, so she already knew what had happened. She had one side of the story at least. My phone alerted me to another Facebook message from Desmond, but I ignored it.

When I arrived home, Miranda was waiting there for me. She was surprised at my makeover. She almost didn't recognize me. She began to laugh once she saw the fake booty I had purchased (note to myself to throw it away). Miranda didn't understand because she had been blessed in that department. Now Ezekiel sleeping with Kiesha and her big butt only made matters worse for my self esteem. The tears started all over again. My makeover didn't make me feel as good as it had earlier. The low self esteem issues started as a child for me.

My parents had me later in life, so I often was dressed old fashioned. I had long thick hair and my mother was unable to take me to the hair dresser so she did the best she could to make it look presentable, but I was picked on a lot because of it. My family didn't have a lot of money, so I couldn't keep up with the latest fashion trends. I often received hand me downs from other cousins and neighbors. My mom shopped at rummage sales or sewed to provide clothing for me. My mom was named Sarai and was around 5 foot 5 inches tall. She had a fair complexion. She had long red hair that she kept in a bun on top of her head. She was a skinny woman. She was beautiful inside and outside. She had a pleasant personality which made it pleasant to be around her.

My dad worked as a janitor. His name was Henry. He was 6 feet tall, dark skinned and his skin looked like chocolate and he had the prettiest white teeth. Daddy kept his head shaved. He was a very attractive man and he loved his wife dearly. If you were around them, you could feel the love they had for one another (just like Ezekiel and I used to be when we first met). He didn't make very much money, but he was a hard worker. He provided a decent living for us. My mom didn't have a job. She stayed at home and raised me until I was school age. She cooked, cleaned, and kept order in the house for dad and me. I may not have had what I wanted but I had everything I needed.

My parents loved me dearly. My clothing often had defects that mom had to sew to help them look better. One day in the winter months, some of the girls were pointing and laughing at a stain on a coat that my mother had gotten for me. I went home crying that day. It is hard growing up with low self-esteem. I had one childhood friend in elementary. We were very close but over the summer, she died suddenly.

My parents thought it would be too traumatic, so they did not take me to the funeral. All I had were memories of her. Mom and dad tried to shelter me from as much as possible. Things that happen to you in your childhood can affect you your entire life. When school began in the fall, there was a new girl in class. I was hoping she would be nice to me. She had moved here from out of state. Her name was Miranda. She overheard the bullying one day and came to my rescue and we have been friends ever since.

I realize now that if I 'd stood up for myself, life for me would have been different. I always took so much negativity from people trying to be friends with any and everyone. I always tried to fit in with the crowd. I was a target for bullies because they knew I never would defend myself or say anything back. That was one reason I was glad to have Miranda around. I remember another cousin that was always so mean to me.

Her name was Angel, but she was no angel. She literally hated my guts. Every opportunity that Angel had to say something cruel or do something cruel to hurt me, she did it. She told me one Christmas that Santa Claus was killed in a plane crash and I would not be receiving any Christmas gifts that year. Moreover, yes, I went home crying again.

The next Christmas she told me that Santa Claus was burned up coming down the chimney and I would not receive any gifts that year either. I never could figure out why she was so evil. She would pick up snakes and insects and play with them. If you got on her bad side, she would throw insects on you and do awful things. Angel told me that if I drank coffee, I would turn black. I never drank coffee and to this day, I still don't drink coffee. I was so gullible.

I believed whatever Angel and anyone else told me. I tried to see the good in Angel but that never lasted long. My mother would ask her to wash my hair whenever she came over and I begged my mom not to ask her to wash my hair, but she never listened. She told me that Angel did not have many friends and since we were family, I should be nice to her. Each time Angel would wash my hair, she would hold my head under the water until I almost passed out and then she would lift my head up. Angel would then make me clean myself up and threatened to kill me if I ever told anyone. I asked her why she was so mean to me and I never did anything to her. She let me know that she hated me for no reason. She said she never liked me, and she never would. She still does not like me.

However, you will be glad to know that one day in my teenage years, I had enough of Angel, and I stood up for myself. Of course, Angel did not like this. We got into the biggest fight. I ended up being victorious in the end. My mom had left to visit a sick friend. Something in me just snapped that day. I beat her up for everything she had ever done to me. She never bothered me anymore after that day. I guess after I finally stood up to her, the fun was gone for her. I found out later that she suffered from a mental illness. I felt sorry for Angel. Even though she was cruel to me, I never wished for anything bad to happen to her. I understood now why she treated me the way she did. She wasn't herself.

But we never talk about mental illness and it does exist. With proper treatment, you can live a productive life. My mom and dad tried to protect me from so many things. I remember one time when I was 12 years old and a relative made a sexual advance towards me. I was so hurt when it happened. He had me cornered off in the kitchen at church. I could not believe he did it at all, let alone at the church. He kept trying to touch me inappropriately and I kept dodging him until finally, someone came around the corner and he took off. I felt so dirty and ashamed. I did not realize at the time that I had not done anything wrong. He was a close relative, so I was hurt by his actions. I avoided him at all costs. My mother began to notice that every time he was around, I would leave or go the other way. She finally asked me about it, and I begin to cry and told her what had happened. My mom went and confronted him about what he had done. Thank God, she did not tell my daddy, because he would have lost his temper. That relative never bothered me anymore after that. I have talked enough about my childhood. It is time to face the problem at hand.

I began to tell Miranda about the events that had happened the day before. She cried too but was the voice of reason. She told me I should give him another chance. She reminded me of the scripture, Romans 3:23 – For all have sinned, and come short of the glory of God. I really didn't want to hear about God or the bible. Ezekiel was not thinking about that when he was with Kiesha. I knew Miranda was right, but I didn't want to hear that. All I kept thinking about was hurting Ezekiel just like he hurt me. I heard a voice say, "vengeance is mine; I will repay, saith the Lord". My faith had gone out of the window at this point. I would come home, cook, clean and run a hot bath for Ezekiel each day he got in from work. Prepare him lunch to take to work with him the next day. I tried to make love to him when time allowed but he was not interested and now I know why, it was because of Kiesha. I served him like the King I thought he was, but it was not good enough. I was angry. No matter how hard I try to do the right thing, it seems like I always get the worse of every situation involving my love life. I thanked Miranda for coming over, but I asked her to leave. I just wanted to be alone. After Miranda left, Ezekiel came home. The girls met him at the door. I just went to our room and shut the door. I begin to cry but I had shed enough tears. Ezekiel thought he was a cheater, but he has not seen anything yet.

Forgiveness

The next few months were a blur to me. Ezekiel begged for forgiveness on a daily basis. I did not have to lift a finger because he did the majority of the housework. He took care of our daughters and he cooked. Ezekiel began writing me love letters. In them, he reminded me of why he fell in love with me. He began catering to me again, but I just could not seem to get past what happened with Kiesha. I tried to call her and cuss her out, but she changed her number. Even if I did get her, she would probably laugh at me. I have never been one to cuss.

However, I could probably come up with some words for her. I thought about telling her husband about what had happened with Ezekiel and her. I do not think anything would come from it because he was cheating on her with another one of our classmates (she just had not found out about it yet). Ezekiel and I started back going to church every Sunday and I just sat there going through the motions. I even went to a life coach. She gave me some good advice and exercises to try at home, but nothing changed on my part. The more I saw Ezekiel, the more I hated him. Every time I looked into those gray eyes, I was reminded of all of the hurt he had caused me. Sex did not exist anymore because every time he tried to make love to me, I saw Kiesha. When we do hurtful things, we never think about the consequences they will have on the people we love. He said he would do anything to win my heart back but the trust in our marriage was gone. It did not help matters, when I got Ezekiel's other cell phone and begin to read go through all the messages and pictures from Kiesha one by one. I guess he didn't think to clear them out.

There were pictures of her in lingerie and in different poses. I took the phone and threw it against the wall. I know it is not healthy to hold things in, but I was just so angry about everything that had happened. After the children were born, I stopped dressing up for bed. The majority of the time I would come to bed with hair rollers and my silk bonnet and gown. Maybe if I would have changed the way I did things, he would not have gone after Keisha. According to the call log, there were times when he was on the phone with her and I was in the same room in our home. I went into a rage.

I grabbed the frame that held our wedding picture and threw it across the room. Glass shattered everywhere. I went into the kitchen and just begin throwing plates and glasses. I grabbed our wedding album and begin to tear picture after picture after picture until I had torn up every single picture. I got a garbage bag and threw away the unity candles from our wedding day, my bouquet, and anything else that was in my sight. I remembered I still had my wedding dress in the closet. I got my scissors, cut it into pieces, and threw away the dress trying to erase any memory of the day I married this man.

During my rage, I received another notification on social media from Desmond. I decided to respond back (what harm could that do). I told him I was married with two kids and was glad to hear from him. He instantly replied back that he was happy to hear from me and we should stay in touch. I thought to myself what harm could this cause.

I was only messaging him on social media. Ezekiel had an affair. He said he had stopped talking to Keisha. He changed his phone number and gave me all of his passwords. He vowed he would never hurt me again. He promised me if I gave him a second chance, he would not betray my trust ever again. He said he would spend the rest of his life making up for the pain he caused me. Ezekiel did not know that I never completely forgave him and vowed to hurt him just as much as he hurt me.

Shannah's Revenge

Ezekiel and I had begun marriage counseling at his suggestion. Things were better in our marriage. The children were especially happy. Everyone was happy but me. It was hard to trust Ezekiel after so much damage had been done. I never believed anything he said anymore. Even though he let me know his every move and was always available for me, I was always suspicious of everything he did. I just kept quiet about how I really felt and went through the motions of marriage. I wanted Ezekiel to hurt just as much as I did. I know the bible tells us to forgive one another and vengeance belongs to God. It just wasn't registering in my mind no matter what I did. I began to talk to Desmond on a daily basis. That made me smile. I thought back to the time when we were in love. I begin to wonder why he contacted me after all of these years. I was so in love with Desmond in school. It didn't hurt that we had known each other since elementary school. Our parents attended church together. Desmond and I ended up breaking up. We just decided it would be best if we ended things, we just were not compatible anymore and we broke up on a good note. He moved away after that and I never heard from him or saw him anymore. Desmond was a nice distraction with all of the chaos that was going on.

Is the grass really greener on the other side of the fence?

Desmond and I communicated a lot on social media. I begin to miss him when I was not messaging him. He began to send messages just to check on me or to let me know I crossed his mind. He told me he had two kids by his ex-wife. He said he also had two kids from a previous relationship. They all had a good friendship because of the children. I told Desmond that he had been busy if he had four children and we both laughed. I told him I was married. I told him about my 2 daughters. The conversations got longer and longer.

Desmond paid attention to me and would listen. That was something Ezekiel had stopped doing was listening. Ezekiel never told me I was pretty. He never asked me how was work. He never asked me how I felt. Ezekiel had it made. He had no worries. He brought me his paycheck and I paid all of the bills. I never spent unnecessary money. I never complained. I always did what was asked of me. Talking to Desmond made me take inventory of my own life. I've always heard the grass was greener on the other side of the fence. I think I will peep over the fence at Desmond and see what happens.

Desmond sent me his phone numbers through social media. He didn't send me just one number, he sent me two numbers. He had two phones (red flag #1). He told me I could contact him at anytime. He said the first phone number was for his business and the next phone number was his personal cell number. I thought it was odd, but Desmond does not lie so having two phones should not be an issue.

We began talking on the phone. He shared things with me about his life. I shared things with him about mine. I vowed never to discuss my husband, but I did (huge mistake). Before I knew it, Desmond and I talked constantly on the phone. I talked to Desmond more than I talked to my family, Miranda, my children and my husband. I started to catch feelings and so did Desmond (mistake #3). I kept right on pretending to be happily married. I went to counseling session after counseling session. I pretended to be happy. I went to school functions with my children and husband and pretended to be happy.

I went to church and pretended to be happy. No one knew the inner battle that was going on inside of me. One day I had had enough, and I told Ezekiel I think we should just get divorced. To my surprise, Ezekiel agreed. He was getting tired of trying to prove to me that he was not cheating anymore. He told me he loved me, and he could not understand why I could not just forgive him and move forward. We met with our attorney and had papers drawn up to proceed with our divorce. Sixty days from today, I would be single again. I would finally be free to live a life free from lies and drama.

Desmond and I continued to talk but we finally agreed it was time to meet in person. We had reconnected and felt it was just time to meet face to face. We choose to meet at the park. I did not think it would hurt to see him.

My gut told me I should not being recently divorced from Ezekiel, but I did not listen. I did not tell Miranda either. I remembered when I was dating Desmond in the past that she never liked him. I decided it was time to make my own decisions and not worry about the outcome. I was going to start thinking about myself for once.

Desmond pulled up in an old beaten down, black Chevrolet truck with paint peeling off and missing hubcaps (he told me he owned a Mercedes). He looked flawless. He looked so good that it took my mind off the old truck that he was driving. The sweet but musk scent of his cologne was not too strong but just delicate enough to linger in your nostrils. He smelled so wonderful. He demanded your attention. He was wearing Louis Vuitton pants, shirt with the matching belt and boots. He had a Rolex. He had a bald head and was clean shaven. My mouth was literally watering.

I had to shake myself to keep from staring. He had matured a lot since we last saw each other. He was staring at me the same way I was looking at him. I did not look like the same girl from school. My new makeover was really working for me and I was now turning heads just like Miranda. I wore an olive-green halter dress that came halfway up my long legs with a cute pair of strappy wedge sandals. I wore red MAC lip gloss and red nail and toe polish. My new blonde hair really complimented my skin tone.

I knew I looked flawless. He complimented me on my new look, and I thanked him. I complimented him as well. Desmond told me his car was in the shop and he had to bring one of his work trucks. I took his word for it. He had a picnic basket in his hand. He said he had prepared us some sandwiches, fruit and bottled water. He knew I had been forgetting to eat with all that was going on in my life and he said he just wanted to share a meal with me. Desmond was so thoughtful. My mind went back to when Ezekiel and I first met and how he would cater to me, but I promised myself I would not play the comparison game. Desmond and I walked to a table in the middle of the park under the trees and he and I ate and talked. Desmond now knew how unhappy I had been and agreed to help me find a place to stay.

Desmond was a private investigator and he had Ezekiel investigated. Ezekiel was not as faithful as he said he was. The report showed Ezekiel had another woman he was also involved with and she was pregnant. He had pictures of this female. This sealed the deal for me, even though I was divorced; I realized my marriage was truly over.

Desmond even told me that he prayed to God for me. He had been asking God for me for years. He had heard I was unhappy (red flag #2). Desmond told me that God had given us a second chance to be together and we had to act on it now. We were having such a good time catching up with each other that we lost track of time. When we realized how late it had gotten. We both parted ways. Neither one of us wanted to leave but we had too.

Desmond had asked me to start a life with him and that I would never have to worry about money. He said some investment deals were very successful and he had hundreds of thousands of dollars buried if he ever hit hard times. He even offered to take me to where it was. He said it was about an hour away. The money is in a garden that his family owned. He said he was going to dig it up and bring it with him but the backhoe he was going to rent to break the ground up was already rented out that day (another red flag I ignored). I think I will move forward with Desmond. After all, of the drama with Ezekiel it will be good to have a fresh start.

Desmond's story seemed to add up. He purchased me a very nice condominium. It was fully furnished. I did not have any worries. He even gave me a debit card to use. Life just could not be any better. He did all of this and I had not even slept with him. He said as soon as he was able to rent the backhoe and dig up the money he had stashed away, he would purchase me a vehicle so I would not have to drive the one Ezekiel had purchased.

He had been saving money for years and was just waiting on me. He would provide all my needs and I could start picking out house designs. He said when I was ready, we would get married, build a house and he would take care of my children. Sounds good does not it (but like my mommy always said, "anything that sounds too good to be true usually is").

He began giving me money, buying me clothes and jewelry. He often had to spend time out of town when he had cases. This was not an issue because I was already used to being alone since Ezekiel was a truck driver. He changed companies once I found out about Kiesha. Ezekiel and I communicated better since our divorce was final. We had talked to our daughters about the divorce and often reminded them that it was not their fault. My daughters wanted me to work it out with their dad.

I told them they were too young to understand. I told them they had to live with the both of us in separate homes. People were wondering, how we could divorce and live and share custody of our children. I do not know how I was able to do it myself, but I did. Ezekiel never missed an opportunity to apologize and let me know that he still loved me. He would send flowers to my job. He would text and let me know I much of a blessing I was to him and how thankful he was I was the mother of his children. I told him it was a little too late. I was not in love with him anymore and it was best we just move forward with our lives. I never told him about Desmond (but he would find out who he was soon enough).

Desmond and I were so great together. He was the perfect guy. We saw each other as often as we could. He had given me all of his passwords because he said he had nothing to hide. Everything was perfect for a month. I begin to pay attention to Desmond's routine. He would drop by and bring me some food and leave. His phone rang the entire time he was with me, but he never answered it. When I questioned him, he said it could wait, that I was more important. Desmond told me that I had his undivided attention. He always had an excuse to leave.

He said he was working cases and when his cases slowed down, he would be able to stay longer. I went along with his story. So for the next month, I went to work, came home to an empty house when I did not have visitation with my children. I begin to wonder; did I make a mistake. I didn't complain since all of my needs were being met. I decided to talk to Desmond about how lonely I was since I was not with Ezekiel anymore. Desmond was supposed to take me out to dinner tonight and I decided I would talk to him after dinner.

Desmond called and said he had to work a case and couldn't take me to dinner, but he would just bring me some food. I went to get some gas in my car (the one Ezekiel was paying for). The credit card Desmond gave me was declined. I knew that couldn't be right, so I did what we all do in those situations, I swiped the card again and it was declined. Desmond had some explaining to do. Thank God, I still had the credit card Ezekiel gave me for emergencies and it worked.

Desmond did not make it to the house until late that night and I was angry. He wouldn't take my calls. He didn't answer my text messages. The same cycle I had with Ezekiel began with Desmond.

The grass is not greener on the other side

Desmond informed me that he had to go to Dallas, TX for the weekend. He asked me to travel with him. At first, I hesitated. After his credit card declined, I was wondering did he have all of the money he claimed to have. I asked him about his credit card declining and he told me he had to cancel the card because the account was frozen because of an unpaid student loan he had.

I thought this was strange but surely, he wouldn't lie about something like that. He promised me he would give me another card to another account he had because he did not want me using Ezekiel's card. I was worried about people seeing Desmond and I together. Ezekiel wanted to keep our divorce private. I think that's because he was still trying to win my heart back, but people would find out sooner or later. But if Desmond wasn't seeing anyone and neither was I, it shouldn't be a problem. I told Desmond that I would go to Dallas with him.

I called Miranda but she didn't answer. I left her a voicemail that I would be in Dallas for the weekend with Desmond in case anything happened to me and someone would know my whereabouts. This was so out of character for me. I never went anywhere without my family. I always had my children or husband with me. But it's a first time for everything.

Desmond pulled up in a rental car. I was hoping to ride in the Mercedes he owned. He informed me it was in the shop for repairs. Desmond always pulled up in different vehicles with different license plates. Some of the license plates were from different states. When I questioned him about that, he said they were work vehicles. I begin writing down the license plates to all of the different vehicles he drove. I have trust issues now so one day I may have to verify if what Desmond is telling me is the truth. But I'm not going to think about that today because I'm off to Dallas to enjoy the weekend.

I know this will sound strange, but I never traveled outside of New Orleans. I was born and raised here and guess I will always be here. He promised to buy me a pair of Christian Louboutin (red bottoms). I can't wait to get them. With my makeover and new attitude, I will love wearing them. Desmond told me he only wanted me to have the best of things in life and he would make sure he got only the best for me. He wanted to purchase me a bottle of Tom Ford perfume. He always seemed to have my best interest at heart. As I was riding, I begin to think about my divorce from Ezekiel. He was the only man I had ever been with. Desmond and I had discussed about being intimate. He said he would wait until I was ready. I was hoping he didn't bring it up this weekend because I wasn't ready yet. I did feel like he didn't want to wait much longer.

Things had become pretty heated between the both of us. I didn't want to rush things though being newly divorced. But enough of daydreaming I began to focus back on Desmond. The drive to Dallas was nice. We stopped to fill up in a town that was famous for its barbeque. Desmond went in to pay for the gas and purchased us a plate with a variety of meat with different sauces. The food was delicious. I wondered why he only purchased one plate, but he told me we would share the plate because that would be more romantic. So I fed Desmond while he drove, and we talked the entire drive. I didn't realize how much we had in common.

We pulled up to the hotel. The valet came and took our luggage and moved the car for us. When we went to check in, I begin to get nervous. So many questions begin to run through my mind. Was Desmond going to try to be intimate with me? I was in a town where I didn't know anybody, would he try to hold me hostage? All kind of thoughts were going through my head. I was beginning to wonder should I have taken this trip. We went up to our room and to my relief, there were double beds. Desmond said he felt that I wasn't ready and reassured me that he was a gentleman and would wait until I was ready. He said he saw how nervous I was and wanted me to just relax. I was so glad he sensed this. I could relax now.

It was something how he always knew what to say to calm my nerves. After he changed clothes, we headed to the mall. We went to purchase my red bottoms. When we walked in the store, he informed the sales clerk that he wanted to purchase me a pair of red bottoms. She came and measured my foot to determine the correct size. Desmond told me if they had my size, he would have to leave and transfer some money into his account to complete the purchase. I thought this was strange but went with the flow. Unfortunately for me, they didn't have my size. Desmond told me not to worry because he would order me a pair online now that we knew what size I wore. We left the mall and went to a famous restaurant in the city. We had a romantic candle light dinner.

There was soft music playing in the background. I wore a white fitted strapless dress. Desmond ordered my food for me. Everything was delicious. I had the prime rib and he had a steak. I was so full, I couldn't eat dessert. The evening was going so lovely. When the waiter came to bring us the bill, Desmond pulled out his black card. It's so nice to be with someone and not have to worry about money.

Desmond was all the things that Ezekiel wasn't. I was already head over hills in love and he was just making it easier to fall for him with all of the special attention. The waiter returned rather quickly and informed Desmond that his card had been declined. This confused me, if Desmond had all of the money, he claimed to have then why was his card being declined. He had a story for why the card had declined just like any other thing I asked him about. He said he had to use that card to pay for the hotel room and they had placed a hold on it, and it was not enough money to cover the meal. He pulled out another card and thankfully it went through. I'm beginning to wonder if Desmond is really who he says he is.

I always try to see the good in everyone, so I put all of the red flags about Desmond behind me and focused on the wonderful night we were having. I had never been with anyone but Ezekiel but with all of the special attention Desmond was showing to me and getting the condominium, I felt like I owed it to him to be intimate with him. I told Desmond that when we got back to the hotel, I wanted him to make love to me. He asked me was I sure and I told him I was. By the time we made it up to the room, my nervousness had returned. Desmond said he was going to shower and told me to relax. When he went into the bathroom, his phone started buzzing. He told me he had turned his ringer off because the weekend would be about us and he wasn't taking any phone calls and giving me his undivided attention.

His phone kept buzzing, so my curiosity got the best of me and I decided to go through it.

I noticed he had been messaging random females on social media. He sent them the same message he had sent me. There were multiple phone calls and voice mails. His ex-wife was at the top of the list. One voicemail was alarming. It was the property owner to the condominium; he said Desmond was 3 months behind on rent. He would be getting an eviction notice, if he did not pay the rent he owed. I was dumbfounded. He told me he purchased the condominium free and clear. I left one liar for another one. I was so upset and hurt. I guess it serves me right. I should have had Desmond investigated before falling in love with him. I begin to cry. I thought Desmond was the one. I guess I should have moved a little slower before jumping into another relationship with another man so soon after my divorce. I grabbed my things and left. I didn't know where I was or what I was going to do. I walked to the restaurant next door to the hotel and called Miranda. Lucky for me she answered. She fussed at me about the voicemail I had left her. She asked me why did

I leave and I barely knew anything about Desmond, and he could've did harm to me and no one would have known where to find me. I told her I needed help and didn't need to hear any of what she was saying at the moment. I told her I needed her to wire me some money so I could come home. Miranda surprised me by what she said next. She was in Dallas. She asked me to let her know my location and she would come and get me. I started crying again. Miranda was my true friend. It didn't matter that we disagreed about Desmond, she would always come and see about me. She told me that when she got my voicemail, she drove out to Dallas and rented a hotel room because she had a feeling, I was in over my head and would need her help. I told her my location and waited on her to come and pick me up. I knew this would be a long ride back home. Desmond called me constantly and I kept refusing his phone calls. During his calls, I checked my email and the private investigator I hired to investigate Desmond had sent me a report of his findings. What I saw literally shocked me. I powered my phone off and went to sleep once I was in Miranda's room.

I knew I would have to deal with him and everyone else when I got back home. When I got back from Dallas, Desmond was waiting for me at the condominium and I confronted him about everything. He told me that he didn't buy the condo but was renting to own it. He said the reason the credit card declined was because his bank accounts had been frozen because his ex girlfriend that worked at the bank had hacked into his accounts and transferred money into a separate account under a different name.

She confessed to him earlier that day and she could possibly lose her job. The bank was investigating her for fraud and since his bank account had been linked to her, they had frozen his accounts too. Too many things were surfacing about Desmond that I didn't like. He would always bring a different vehicle each time he came over. I questioned him and he said that two of the vehicles were his business vehicles. He did surveillance work and he couldn't use his personal vehicle.

I was tired of the back and forth with Desmond. I told him I had hired a private investigator and the report showed he was married with 5 children by his wife. He had an additional 8 children with 5 other women. He lived with his parents.

The vehicles belonged to his wife and his baby momma's. He really had 13 children instead of the four he told me about (he claimed that one of the four children were not his but since he was such a good man, he supported the child anyway). He had a criminal record and he was bankrupt. If he had all of this money buried, I do not understand why he would not dig it up and pay off his debts. I confronted Desmond about the report on him. He admitted he hadn't been totally honest with me. He said he was divorced, and he would show me his divorce papers. He said he didn't tell me about all of his children because he was scared, I would think he had too many children. What kind of man would lie about his children?

Desmond said that when he first started talking to me, he only wanted to get back at Ezekiel for sleeping with his girlfriend in high school. He made up a fake report on Ezekiel because he knew I would not leave him completely without some type of proof. He lied about the other woman. He said the vehicles were his but he got the tag in another state under his relative name so he would not have to pay taxes. I was so angry. My mind was going in several different directions with everything Desmond had just revealed to me. I did not know what to believe. He was such a liar that you could not trust anything he said. I was so caught up in getting revenge on Ezekiel until I was blinded by what I thought was love.

I had isolated myself from my family and my best friend all for Desmond. I didn't listen to the warnings. I begin to cry again. Desmond apologized and begged me for forgiveness. He said God wanted us together. He had been praying for me and there were too many signs that we should be together, but he went about it the wrong way but just give him another chance to make it right. I heard a car pull up in the driveway and it was Ezekiel. I instantly panicked. I knew he carried a gun on him at all times and I was suddenly afraid.

He didn't know about Desmond, but he was about to find out about him. Ezekiel knocked on the door and I told Desmond to go in the bedroom. I went to the door and asked him how did he find out where I was. He said he had been following me. He told me he knew about Desmond and if I would just come home, all would be forgotten and forgiven. Desmond came into the room where Ezekiel and I were. Ezekiel told him he knew who he was. My heart begins to race. Ezekiel told Desmond he wanted me back and would stop at nothing to get me back. He asked me to come back home. I told him no. It was too much damage done at this point.

Desmond begins to brag to Ezekiel that he had so much money in the bank, he had purchased me this condominium, and he had multiple businesses. On the inside I'm thinking, "Didn't you get an eviction notice". Suddenly, Ezekiel threw a punch at Desmond. It knocked him out cold. Ezekiel told me to get my stuff because he was taking me home. I was afraid at this point because he had never been so angry with me. Ezekiel and I left but not together. He thought I was behind him, but I took a detour.

I got a phone call and answered without looking at the caller I.D. and it was a female's voice. She said her name was Lucinda and she was Desmond's wife. She said she just wanted me to listen. Lucinda said she wasn't calling to be messy. She began to tell me that Desmond was the devil in disguise, and I wasn't the only one he had lied to. Lucinda told me about the recent events that had went on with us so I knew then that she wasn't lying because how else would she had known. She said Desmond tells anyone he wants to have a relationship with that he is divorced, but they aren't. She asked me did he ever show me any divorce papers (I guess that was the reason he kept forgetting to show them to me). Lucinda said Desmond was obsessed with getting revenge on Ezekiel for the one night stand they had when they were in high school (I didn't know he knew Ezekiel before now). She said he had 2 other females in two other states, set up just like he had me set up and that is why he doesn't have any money. She told me he is constantly in and out of jail because of unpaid child support. Lucinda said she would never divorce Desmond either, because she loved him and she cheated too, so she considered them to be even.

I guess getting even doesn't feel as good as I thought it would. I just hung up the phone and didn't say anything to her. Tears just flooded down my face and before I realized it, I had driven to a popular walking track that is surrounded by water. I pulled up and sat there and begin to think about all of the things that had happened to me. Maybe I should've worked things out with Ezekiel. I tried to get even but that didn't work. I ended up getting played. Desmond lied about everything. A friend of mine often referred to their relatives as professional liars. I think Desmond fits this description. I thought back to when I was younger and my mother told me that the devil's job is to steal, kill and destroy. Desmond really was the devil in disguise. I was trying so hard to get even with Ezekiel until I was blinded by the lies. I let the devil destroy me. I was now divorced from my husband. I felt as though I had nothing left to live for. I had no money. I had no place to go. That was my first mistake, shutting myself off from the people that loved me. I had stopped talking to my parents. They told me I should work things out with Ezekiel. They also advised me to take some time and find myself again and it was too soon to start a new relationship after being married and having children by my ex husband.

After those comments, I didn't talk to them anymore. Being blinded, like so many others, I started to keep to myself. As long as I had

Desmond, I thought I didn't need anyone else. Red flags should have gone up then, but I ignored them. Desmond pulled me away from the people that loved me and had my best interest at heart. He told me that as long as we had each other, we didn't need anyone else. I believed everything he told me. I can't blame Desmond for everything because I let him do it. I know that nothing that starts out wrong will end up right. But I took a chance. I had grown up always praying and reading my bible and I became a victim to the same games that so many other women had. I pulled the gun from under my seat and looked at it. The feel of the cold metal against the palm of my hand sent shivers throughout me. I know suicide isn't the answer, but I felt I couldn't come back from all of the bad choices I had made. As the tears filled my eyes, I begin to replay my entire life. My child hood flashed before my eyes. I remembered the bullying and how I never stood up for myself. I see how easy it was for Desmond to deceive me. I didn't realize that he was weak himself and he was a bully too. I thought about the constant need to be perfect in all that I did.

If I killed myself, at least my suffering would be over. Everything went from bad to worse in my life, so I didn't see the point of living anymore. My daughters would be better off without me. How could I have been so stupid. I felt embarrassed about how my situation ended. What would people say when they found out? If I am dead, I won't live to find out what they will say. I put the gun up to my head, closed my eyes and pulled the trigger. After a few minutes had passed, I realized I was still alive. I pulled the clip out and realized there were no bullets in the clip. I couldn't even kill myself right. I begin to cry again until I heard a voice say, "I'm still here". I looked around because I knew I was alone. I heard a voice say again, "I never left you, you left me". I've always had a close relationship with God and a strong prayer life before Desmond. I heard a voice say, "we all have sinned and fell short of the glory of God". My whole life I tried to live perfect. I always did what my parents asked and followed all the rules in school. In church, I always did what was asked of me. In my marriage, I always did what Ezekiel wanted. Somewhere along the line, I lost myself. It is sad it took me trying to end my life for me to find myself. I often wondered how so many women ended up in some of the circumstances they did. It was easy being so judgmental of other people when you haven't walked in their shoes. I now know myself how easy it is to be deceived.

This was a hard lesson for me, but everything happens for a reason. So from this day forward, I am going to work on finding Shannah. I repented of my sins and asked God to forgive me. Thank God for second chances. I thanked God for sparing my life in the midst of my sins. I am trusting God to direct my path and I know I won't go wrong as long as he is leading me. I remember a scripture in the bible that says, "Vengeance is mine". I think from here on out I will let God fight my battles for me. I know that getting even isn't the answer. If you are ever in a relationship, don't get so caught up with the other person until you lose sight of reality. And lastly, if your inner voice is telling you something is wrong, please listen to that inner voice. I had multiple opportunities to end things with Desmond, but I ignored all of the signs. I felt like I owed him something.

In reality, I didn't owe him anything. He always asked me did I trust him, and of course I said yes. He just was preying on my nurturing nature. But I can't let this one bad experience stop me from having another relationship. I must learn from it, share with others so it will not happen to them, and remember so it will not happen to me again.

6 months later (what goes around, comes back around)

Miranda invited me to attend a workshop offered at the local library on how to start a successful business. She encouraged me to start my own business doing something I loved. She knew I had been through a lot with Ezekiel and Desmond. I agreed to go to the workshop with her. Everything was going great and I was learning a lot of new things in order to start a business. They had a guest speaker that was about to come up and talk about their business.

When I looked up and saw the speaker come from the back room to the podium, my mouth literally dropped open. It was Desmond, and he looked flawless. He had grown his hair out. He was wearing short dreadlocks. It was such a change for him, but they looked good on him. He was wearing a designer suit, shoes, Rolex watch and diamond ring. It always seems like the ones that do the most harm always end up with the most. Desmond was a professional liar (someone who tells so many lies until it sounds like the truth). As I sat there and looked at him, I thought back to everything that had happened with us. The sparks I thought I felt with him were gone. There was no attraction and I just genuinely felt sorry for him. I guess what I thought was love was lust. As he began to talk, I stopped daydreaming and begin listening to what he was saying. Desmond always had a way with words. He had the power of persuasion and he used it to his advantage. He was telling how successful his private investigator business was and the struggles he had starting it. He did not see me because I sat in the back of the room. He bragged about all of the money he had and all the material things he had gained. I was shocked. He didn't mention his wife or all of his children not once. I was trying to keep my composure and not bring attention to us. Miranda was elbowing me so hard. The lady that was sitting in front of us was also discussing Desmond with the lady sitting next to her. She said that Desmond was the father of her child (oh my God this makes number 14) but he denied being her father even after DNA testing. Just when I thought I had Desmond figured out, here comes another bombshell. I am so glad that I do not have to be worried about him anymore. She then said she was calling the police because he had a warrant for unpaid child support for their child. Miranda and I were shocked. Desmond was bragging about how much money he had, and he couldn't afford to pay his child support. About 10 minutes passed and just as Desmond was walking toward his seat sitting down on the stage, several police officers walked up to the podium, placed handcuffs on him, read him his rights and escorted him out of the library. On his way out, he looked over to the direction of where I was sitting, and our eyes met. He looked shocked and embarrassed. Maybe he should go and dig up the money he supposedly has buried. I knew it was wrong, but a big smile came on my face and I begin to laugh. I hope he has learned his lesson. *To be continued.*

www.ingramcontent.com/pod-product-compliance
Lightning Source LLC
Chambersburg PA
CBHW070450170726
48291CB00005B/1684

9781949888669